PUFFIN BOOKS

The Coldest Day in the Zoo

Alan Rusbridger lives in London with a family that includes, a wife, two daughters, a dog called Angus and a cat called Retro. He has forgotten why the cat is called Retro. He also edits the *Guardian*.

D0177143

ALAN RUSBRIDGER

The Coldest Day in the Zoo

Illustrated by Ben Cort

PUFFIN

PUFFIN BOOKS

Published by the Penguin Group
Penguin Books Ltd, 80 Strand, London WC2R 0RL, England
Penguin Group (USA), Inc., 375 Hudson Street, New York, New York 10014, USA
Penguin Books Australia Ltd, 250 Camberwell Road, Camberwell,
Victoria 3124, Australia
Penguin Books Canada Ltd, 10 Alcorn Avenue, Toronto, Ontario, Canada M4V 3B2
Penguin Books India (P) Ltd, 11 Community Centre, Panchsheel Park,
New Delhi – 110 017, India
Penguin Books (NZ) Ltd, Cnr Rosedale and Airborne Roads,
Albany, Auckland, New Zealand
Penguin Books (South Africa) (Pty) Ltd, 24 Sturdee Avenue,
Rosebank 2196, South Africa

Penguin Books Ltd, Registered Offices: 80 Strand, London WC2R 0RL, England

www.penguin.com

First published 2004
3

Text copyright © Alan Rusbridger, 2004
Illustrations copyright © Ben Cort, 2004
All rights reserved

The moral right of the author and illustrator has been asserted

Set in Bembo

Made and printed in England by Clays Ltd, St Ives plc

British Library Cataloguing in Publication Data
A CIP catalogue record for this book is available from the British Library

ISBN 0–141–317450

For Tib and Lizzie

Chapter One

It was slap bang in the middle of the coldest day of the coldest week of the year that the central heating broke down at Melton Meadow Zoo.

Worse still, the coldest day happened to be a Friday. The central heating repair man was called. He poked, rattled and rumbled around for an age and announced that he couldn't  possibly mend it before Monday. The system needed something called a new flange. Flanges were not to be obtained on a Friday afternoon in midwinter in Melton Meadow. 'Are you sure?'

enquired a shivering Mr Pickles, the head keeper, who wasn't quite sure what a flange was, but didn't like to ask.

'Quite sure,' said the central heating repair man cheerily. 'See you on Monday. That will be twenty-two pounds thirty, please.'

Mr Pickles shivered again and shook his head. How, he wondered, was he supposed to look after the animals all weekend? He looked out of his window and saw that they were already beginning to feel the cold.

The lion's teeth were ch-ch-ch-chattering. The penguin was flapping

his wings and bouncing up and down
on the spot, which made Mr Pickles
feel rather giddy. The anaconda had
wrapped herself around the flex
above the light, so as to be near the
warm bulb.

Only the polar bear was chirpy and, I'm afraid to say, couldn't resist walking past some of the shivering animals with an unmistakably smug look on his face. The others glared back just a shade sourly. But not too sourly, because they remembered only too well the long, hot summer days when they'd done just the same to the sweltering bear.

Mr Pickles surveyed all this and the solution came to him in a flash. He called all the keepers into his room and explained the problem. 'The central heating is broken,' he said. 'It's

er, um, a flange. And Melton Meadow
is all out of flanges until Monday
morning.'

The keepers shook their heads in a
worried sort of way. They didn't
know what a flange was either, nor
did any of them like to ask.

'So,' said Mr Pickles, 'what we have
to do is this: each keeper must take his

or her animal home with them for the weekend, keep them warm and then bring them back again on Monday morning. Any questions?'

The news came as such a surprise that none of the keepers could think of a question. And so they all trooped off to pick up their animals.

And this is the story of what happened to some of those keepers and animals that frosty weekend in Melton Meadow …

Chapter Two

Mr Pomfrey, the penguin keeper, took his penguin home to his little house in Pumpernickel Lane. Friday night was Mrs Pomfrey's bridge night, when she invited some of her friends around to play cards in the sitting room, so Mr Pomfrey, who was well house-trained, took the penguin straight upstairs to their bedroom. He left him sitting on a blanket on the floor and went downstairs to find something for the penguin's tea. As luck would have it, Mrs Pomfrey had made a delicious fish pie for supper and had a couple of pieces of haddock left over.

Mr Pomfrey went back upstairs to the penguin, gave him the fish and left him to it. This was Mr Pomfrey's first big mistake.

The penguin, who had always hankered after the good life, recognized that this was as near to it as any penguin could decently hope for. He was an emperor penguin – a posh penguin to you and me – and it was a source of some dismay to him that his aristocratic status had never been properly acknowledged by the powers that be at Melton Meadow Zoo.

If he had been living in the wild, he would have lorded it over his fellow penguins. On colder days he would have required them to huddle around him to keep his flippers nice and toasty.

His grandmother had told him all about his noble breeding and this huddling thing. She said it was called a turtle, which had always puzzled him because he was a penguin, not a turtle. He wondered whether, when lots of turtles huddled together, they called it a penguin. But since he was the only penguin in Melton Meadow there was no one to lord it over, or even keep him warm by pretending to be a turtle.

But as he looked around the Pomfreys' bedroom he suddenly felt at home. He gazed in admiration at the bedclothes, the deep purple carpet and the matching bedside lights, and he realized that this was what he had been missing all these years. This was what he had been born to. These were, indeed, surroundings fit for an emperor penguin. He resolved to make himself comfortable. He would start by having tea in bed.

So he picked up his fish supper,
flipped on to the eiderdown,
snuggled under the ample
goosedown duvet Mrs Pomfrey
had recently purchased and
settled down for a nice
meal and a dreamy
snooze.

When Mr Pomfrey
returned an hour later,
night was falling and he could not
see the penguin anywhere, but his

nose told him that something unfortunate had happened. He turned on the light. True enough, there was the penguin, snoring contentedly under the bedclothes. And there were Mrs Pomfrey's new bedclothes, littered with fish bones, smeared with fishy smears and stinking to fishy high heaven.

'Oh no!' groaned Mr Pomfrey. And then: 'Ppffooooooooooor!' as he got nearer and savoured the full impact of the fishy pong.

Holding his nose, he awakened the dozing penguin. 'Come on. Out you get.' And he led the dopey penguin downstairs and left him in the kitchen while he went upstairs to change the sheets and get rid of the smell. This was only partially successful, and for months afterwards Mrs Pomfrey was prone to dreams about haddock and chips.

Leaving the penguin downstairs in the kitchen was Mr Pomfrey's second big mistake. Penguins have sensitive nostrils and I am afraid to say that Mr Pomfrey's penguin was quick to realize that there was yet more fish to be had. His nose took him to a dish sitting on the kitchen surface to the left of the sink. It was just too high to eat where it was, so he niftily swept it on to the floor with a flipper and set about licking the fish pie off the floor, taking care to leave behind the potato topping, which was not to his taste.

By the time Mr Pomfrey came downstairs the penguin was sitting happily on the floor, preening his feathers and wondering what more life had to offer. The immediate answer to this was being banished to

the potting shed, where he was forced to spend a night in conditions he did not consider remotely befitting a noble emperor penguin. Though Mr Pomrey did supply him with a blanket and a paraffin stove.

It would be kinder not to dwell on Mrs Pomfrey's reaction when her bridge evening ended and she emerged to find the whole house ponging of fish and Mr Pomfrey clumsily trying to knock up a supper out of some old sausages he'd found stuck behind a mouldy lettuce in the fridge.

All in all, the weekend was not a great success.

Chapter Three

Mr Emblem, the elephant keeper, took his elephant home with him to his house in Enderby Drive. Now, of course, it had never occurred to Mr Emblem that he would ever have occasion to entertain an elephant at home, or else he would have bought a larger house. As it was, he had bought a small house. Too small for an

elephant. And it was some way from
Melton Meadow Zoo. Too far for an
elephant to walk. Or, at any rate, too
far for an elephant who was a touch
out of condition. So, by the time the
pair of them made it to Enderby
Drive, both were a tiny bit grumpy.

Mr Emblem had been plotting on
his way home. Though the house

was small, it had a big garage and Mr Emblem had a small car. So – he figured as he tried to avoid the curious stares of passers-by – there would be plenty of room for the elephant in the garage as well as a car.

This was Mr Emblem's first big mistake.

Mr Emblem left the elephant in the garage and went off to get her some food.

The elephant, weary after the long walk from the zoo, decided to sit down. She sat on the car. The car was squashed.

Not only squashed but flattened. It is a little known fact that an elephant can weigh up to six times the weight of a car. On this occasion, it was no contest. Mr Emblem's shiny Mini – second-hand, but still his pride and joy – was as flat as a pancake.

'Oh no!' groaned Mr Emblem when he returned and saw the elephant sitting smugly on a bed of mangled Mini. And then 'G r r r r r r r r r r !', which was his way of telling the elephant he was not entirely pleased with her.

'Come on,' he said. 'Out!'

And he led the elephant into the back garden, with a duvet over her head to keep her warm. It is probably best to pass over the subsequent incident, which involved a water butt, a quantity of icy water, the elephant's trunk and an astonished neighbour.

Two hours later a local scrap dealer came round and took away the pile of twisted metal that had once been Mr Emblem's pride and joy.

The elephant was allowed back into the garage, where she remained for the next forty-eight hours.

All in all, the weekend was not a great success.

Chapter Four

Mrs Crumble, the crocodile keeper, took her crocodile home to the small house she shared with Mr Crumble in Cross-stitch Crescent. On her way home she pondered the best place to keep the crocodile since, as you know, they like to split their lives between living on land and living in water.

She decided the best place to keep him would be in the bathroom which was a nice big room. She would fill the bath with pleasantly warm water and the crocodile could decide whether to lie on the tiles or in the bath itself.

This was Mrs Crumble's first big mistake.

As luck would have it, Friday night was the evening that Mr Crumble came home late from work. It was also the evening that Mrs Crumble went to her evening class in lawn mower maintenance. Before she went out, she fed the crocodile, led him upstairs to the bathroom and scribbled a note for Mr Crumble, which she left on the kitchen table.

Mrs Crumble was getting quite good at maintaining lawn mowers, but she was still not very good at spelling. She was considering trying spelling night classes once she had finished with lawn mowers.

The note read:

Diner in the uven. Bewaire.
Crock in bath.

Mr Crumble returned home and read the scribbled note in the absent-minded sort of way that he had. He was long accustomed to Mrs Crumble's eccentric fashion with spelling.

A what in the bath? He puzzled vaguely. A clock in the bath? That didn't sound right. A frock in the bath? That seemed very unlikely. A crack in the bath? That was bothersome.

He would have to call the plumber. Whereupon he forgot all about it and settled down to watch the news on television.

After the news he went upstairs and started running the bath. He was still distracted by Mrs Crumble's mysterious note, and he quite failed to notice that the bath was already half-full.

The Friday Night Bath was Mr Crumble's favourite moment of the week. With Mrs Crumble out of the house, he could pamper himself rotten. So this week, as with every other week, he lit some scented

candles, selected his favourite bubble
bath oil and began to sing to himself,

quietly at first, then a little less quietly.

So absent-minded was he that he had quite forgotten all about clocks, frocks and cracks – and entirely failed to notice the croc.

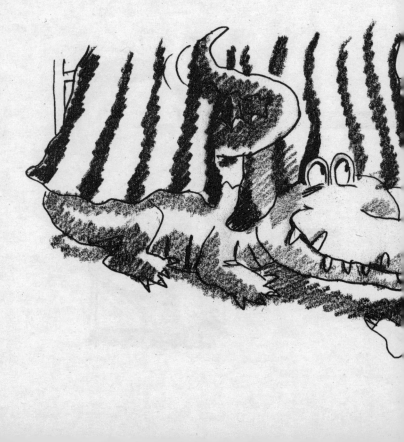

The croc, however, had not failed to notice him.

From his vantage point under the heated towel rail he eyed Mr Crumble (who was now undressing)

with some disdain and decided he
would have the bath first. As Mr
Crumble lit his final scented candle
the croc slipped unnoticed beneath
the bubbles.

The first that Mr Crumble
knew of anything was as
he lowered himself into
the tub. SNAP! The
crocodile bit Mr Crumble
on the bottom.

'AA – ooo – ow!'
yelled Mr Crumble,
leaping out of
the bath.

He turned round and saw a green and disgruntled figure emerging menacingly from a mass of foam.

'A croc!' he said. 'A croc in the bath. Why on earth didn't she say so?'

And with that he fled downstairs stark naked, slamming the bathroom door behind him.

'Oh no!' said Mrs Crumble when she returned from her evening class and found Mr Crumble – hiding beneath the kitchen table without any clothes on. And then 'Hrumph!', which was her way of telling the crocodile he had misbehaved something rotten.

And then she led the crocodile out into the garden while she stuck a sticking plaster on Mr Crumble's bottom.

'You can just stay out there for a bit to cool off,' she said severely.

Taking the crocodile out into the garden was Mrs Crumble's second big mistake. For in the middle of an immaculately mown lawn (courtesy of Mrs Crumble and her hand-renovated eighteen-inch Suffolk Punch mower) was an ornamental pond, surrounded by little gnomes and stocked with Mr Crumble's precious pet fish collection.

To most people one fish is much like another fish. Mr Crumble was not most people. Mr Crumble had spent his life building up his fish collection. He did not bother with mundane goldfish. He was, truth to tell, something of a fish snob, and many was the argument he had had with Mrs Crumble over the amount of money lavished on his fish which could have been better spent on curtains, foreign holidays or lawn mowers. His life savings had gone into the most exotic species he could find. He had, over the years, specialized in carp: koi carp, bronze carp, Prussian carp, red carp, leather carp and – some said – the biggest collection of mirror carp outside Japan.

In the summer he had a Pond Open Day and fish-fanciers came from as far afield as Macclesfield in order to admire his fish.

The crocodile knew none of this, and cared even less. He was still most put out from being disturbed in his bath and rather rudely ordered to wait outside while Mr Crumble's bottom received medical attention.

Spotting the pond, he thought this would be an excellent opportunity to wash off the Essence of Hyacinth bubble bath with which he had been coated.

So, ignoring the little gnomes, he slithered into the icy water of the pond. There, he cooled off nicely and then perked up no end when he saw

Mr Crumble's life work swimming in front of his eyes.

He had been wrong to think bad thoughts about Mrs Crumble, he reflected. She was right to patch up her husband's bottom. And she was so thoughtful to lay on such a delicious fresh fish supper.

He was a well-brought up crocodile and did not rush. Each mouthful was rolled around the tongue and savoured before slipping down his gullet. By the time Mrs Crumble came out the crocodile was on to his last little silver bream carp. And very tasty it was too.

All in all, the weekend was not a great success.

Chapter Five

Mr Raja, the rhino keeper, took his rhino home to his semi-detached house in Rumbold Road and placed him in the sitting room, which was the largest room in the house and thus, thought Mr Raja, the most suitable. A kindly man, Mr Raja did not wish the rhino to become bored and so he switched on the television to keep him happy while he went to the kitchen to get him some supper.

This was Mr Raja's first big mistake.

Mr Raja thought he would leave the rhino with something calming, yet educational. So he avoided *EastEnders*, the Shopping Channel and MTV and switched on a demonstration of knitting techniques on Channel Four. The rhino gazed at it with moderate interest. But while Mr Raja was out of the room the knitting programme ended, to be followed by a wildlife programme.

As luck would have it, the subject that week was rhinos.

Pretty soon, there were rhinos all

over the screen. Running rhinos, feeding rhinos, swimming rhinos, grunting rhinos. Mr Raja's rhino sat up and grunted back at the television. The television rhinos responded by grunting back most provocatively – or so he thought.

Mr Raja's rhino was normally well behaved and did not stand on dignity. But nor did he take kindly to being dissed by other rhinos to whom he had not even been introduced. He grunted and, I'm sorry to say, started pawing Mr Raja's brand new carpet.

He was just about to write off the other rhinos as beneath contempt, and thus not worth bothering with, when a bunch of them started running straight towards him, heads

bowed, horns like lances. Mr Raja's rhino could take it no more. He leapt up, pawed fearsomely at the carpet, snorted fearsomely through inflamed nostrils. And charged.

A rhino and a television set is not a fair fight. Consider the statistics.

Weight: Rhino – One and a half tonnes
TV – 25 kilograms

Length: Rhino – three metres five centimetres
TV – 56 centimetres

Charging Speed: Rhino – up to 35 mph
TV – stands still

Length of Horn: Rhino – 52 centimetres
TV – No horn (some have an indoor aerial in place of horn)

The television never stood a chance. There was an almighty crash, a shower of sparks and glass and a plume of smoke. Mr Raja's rhino ran straight through the television set into the wall, knocking out several bricks

before bouncing back and sitting, slightly bewildered, on the carpet. He sniffed the smoke, peered around him, and noted with some satisfaction that the other rhinos appeared to have scarpered. That would teach them, he thought.

Mr Raja heard the explosion and rushed in, looking shocked and astonished. 'Oh no,' he groaned. And then 'RooooooOO!' which was his way of telling the rhino he'd slipped up rather badly in the manners department. Mr Raja's rhino took not a blind bit of notice.

The rhino sat on the sitting room carpet quietly beaming to himself – a beam that said: 'You will have noticed that there is now not one other rhino in sight. I think they realized who was who around here.'

It may be best to pass over the

subsequent incident involving a half-eaten Mars Bar, the gang of local lads rejoicing in the name of the Melton Magpies and a two-mile chase up and down the length of Buttermead Avenue.

All in all, the weekend was not a success.

Chapter Six

Mr Leaf, the lion keeper, took his lion home to his little terraced house in Litigate Lane. This was, you may imagine, not as easy as it sounded. It is not every day that a lion goes for a stroll down the pleasant byways of Melton Meadow. And though Mr Leaf was well known as a very capable lion keeper, and though he kept the lion on a good strong lead, and though the lion appeared to be exceptionally well behaved ... still, many people crossed the street and hid behind pillar boxes and pretended to be gateposts until Mr Leaf and his lion had passed by.

Eventually, the pair

reached home and Mr Leaf decided that he would be best off in the hall, where he could prowl up and down just like he did in the zoo.

This was Mr Leaf's first big mistake.

All went well until Saturday morning. The lion had spent a comfortable night on the hall rug, dozing away like an overgrown guard dog. He was rudely woken by a knock at the door. Mr Leaf answered it, and found Jill the postwoman holding a brown paper parcel. She balanced it under one arm as she got out a piece of paper for Mr Leaf to sign.

Now, as misfortune would have it, it just so happened that the lion's supply of meat arrived at the zoo each day neatly wrapped up by the butcher in a brown paper parcel. The children who came to the zoo loved watching the lion's feeding time: one of the lion's best tricks was to grab the parcel from his keeper and shake off the wrapping before eating the meat. It always brought a round of applause.

Well, the lion saw the postwoman's parcel and put two and two together. That was just like Mr Leaf, he thought. Considerate as ever. He might have brought him to this strange place for the weekend, but he'd been thoughtful enough to make sure his customary supply of meat was personally delivered to the door. First thing too.

He pushed past his keeper, leaped in the air, grabbed the parcel from the postwoman's hand and proceeded to shake it around in his mouth. When he was at the zoo he found he got the best round of applause if he accompanied this trick by letting out a mighty roar. Rrrrrrrrraa-aaaaaaaaurgh! Like so. So now he duly let out one of his most growl-some growls.

During the twenty years

Jill the postwoman had done the job she'd been bitten by dogs as small as gymshoes and as big as a chest of drawers. Dogs no longer held any fear for Jill. She'd even had to cope with the odd goose hissing at her and – on one unforgettable occasion – a llama which had nibbled her left ear.

But being attacked ... in broad daylight ... by what appeared to be a man-eating lion ... on a Saturday morning ... in the middle of Litigate Lane! All this was quite another cup of tea.

She dropped her bag, scattering letters and packages all over the street, and ran for her life. She did not stop running until she made it home on the other side of Melton Meadows. And even then she didn't stop running until she had panted upstairs and locked herself in the lavatory.

It was two days before anyone could persuade her it was safe to leave the lavatory and three weeks before she could be persuaded to go out on her rounds again. And a full three months before she would deliver mail to Mr Leaf.

'Oh no!' groaned Mr Leaf when he
saw Jill the postwoman disappearing
up the road. And then: 'Wrroooomp!',
which was his way of telling the lion

 he was a chump
and he should
know better
by now.
For his
part, the
lion felt more
than a little
foolish since
the parcel, once
he'd unwrapped it, contained nothing
more edible than a set of thermal
underwear Mr Leaf had sent off for in
order to keep out the cold.

That evening Mr Leaf's mother-in-law was coming to supper. Before the meal Mr Leaf took the lion aside and said, 'Now, I don't want you frightening anyone else this weekend, all right? Least of all my mother-in-law. Is that understood?' and he made a little den for the lion behind the sitting-room sofa and gave him a bowl of Horlicks, hoping that he might doze off.

Putting the lion behind the sofa was Mr Leaf's second big mistake.

The Horlicks did the trick and the lion duly nodded off, sleeping right through his own tea-time. He started dreaming about food. He started dreaming he could smell roast beef and Yorkshire pudding.

And then, I am afraid to say, he woke up and realized that he COULD smell roast beef and Yorkshire pudding.

Roast beef and Yorkshire pudding: boy oh boy! An older, wiser lion might at this moment have paused to think. He might have remembered the unfortunate episode with the postwoman and the thermal under-wear. He might have stopped and wondered whether all was quite as it seemed on this strange, shivery cold day.

But Mr Leaf's lion was not yet an old and wise lion. Without pause for any such thoughts, he leaped out from behind the sofa, tore across the sitting room, and in one bound was on top of the dining-room table, sparing no thought at all for the Leafs (plus

mother-in-law), who were just about to say grace.

In no time at all they were flat on their faces while the lion was laying into the roast beef and Yorkshire pudding, not to mention the odd roast potato and parsnip as well.

Mrs Leaf – who was a shy woman at the best of times – was so terrified that she ran out of the house and booked into a hotel for the night. And it was not three days, three weeks or even three months, but three whole years before Mr Leaf's mother-in-law could be persuaded to take dinner in Litigate Lane again. And a good ten years before she could even look at a sirloin steak.

You might be thinking that the weekend was, all in all, not a great success. But it is only fair to record that Mr Leaf took some satisfaction from the following years when his difficult mother-in-law refused to visit. And that, when she eventually did resume her regular trips to Litigate Lane, Mr Leaf occasionally nursed dark thoughts about inviting the lion round too.

Chapter Seven

Never was a Monday morning more warmly welcomed than in the keepers' homes all over Melton Meadow. They were up early and waiting with their animals at the zoo gates when

Mr Pickles, the head keeper, arrived
with the key at nine o'clock.

Never was anyone more relieved
than the keepers were when, shortly
afterwards, the central heating man

arrived with his flange and mended the central heating. Melton Meadow Zoo returned to its cosy self and Mr Pickles said all the keepers could have an extra day off at Christmas as a reward for their weekend's work.

The animals settled back into their normal routines, but life could never be quite the same again.

The penguin had glimpsed the high life. He went to bed dreaming of fish pies and goose eiderdowns.

The elephant – who was a bit of a rebel at heart – had briefly tasted the giddy delights of trashing cars and spraying water at annoying people. Entertaining children would never be quite as much fun again.

The crocodile could not really complain about the food he got at Melton Meadow Zoo. But sometimes, as he fell asleep, he dreamed wistfully of the succulent taste of fresh silver carp and other such delicacies.

And the lion – who eventually grew older and wiser, as we all do – nevertheless enjoyed the odd chuckle as he remembered the astonished expression on the face of Mr Leaf's mother-in-law.

As for the keepers, the first thing they did was to have a collection. With the money they bought two dozen blankets and sixty hot water bottles to keep the animals warm should the heating ever break down again. And, just to be on the safe side, they laid in a plentiful supply of flanges.

They all loved their animals, but one thing they all agreed was that never, ever, EVER again did they want to take them home for the weekend.